Roos in Shoes

These roos in shoes are dedicated to Rory and Alexandra - TK

and to Benedict CASPAR as well - GJ

Random House Australia Pty Ltd
20 Alfred Street, Milsons Point, NSW 2061
http://www.randomhouse.com.au

Sydney   New York   Toronto
London   Auckland   Johannesburg
and agencies throughout the world

First published in hardback by Random House Australia 2003

National Library of Australia
Cataloguing-in-Publication Entry

Keneally, Thomas, 1935- .
       Roos in shoes.

       For primary school children.
       ISBN 1 74051 864 0.

       1. Kangaroos - Juvenile poetry. I. Johnson, Gillian.
       II. Title.

       A821.3

Design: Jobi Murphy
Production: Linda Watchorn
Colour separations: Pica Digital, Singapore
Printer: Tien Wah Press Pte. Ltd., Singapore

Roos in Shoes

Story by Tom Keneally

Pictures by Gillian Johnson

RANDOM HOUSE AUSTRALIA

there is a farm near Cudgedong
to which the kanga tribes belong.
You'll find there every kind of roo:
the grey, and red with females blue.
They crowd in there, close to the ranges
because it keeps them safe from strangers.
The flood plain's farmed by Roger Drewe;
the slopes and grasslands suit the roo.
They like to wave at one another:
the Drewes,
the kangaroos.

the family Drewe grow wheat and clover
in paddocks summer floods wash over.
They make an honest living thus,
and send their daughter on the bus
to school in Callidus.

Some said to gentle Farmer Drewe,
'You ought to put more cattle through,
you ought to have them roaming high
along the hills towards the sky.'
But this was Farmer Drewe's reply:
'There was a time, before Drewes came,
when all the country was the same;
the flood plains and the hills alike,
the rivers full of native pike.
All *that* belonged to kangaroos,
before the coming of the Drewes.
I don't intend to drive the roos
out of the land they love to use,
the land from which they wave to Drewes,
and Drewes wave too.'

then one day came another threat
that caused the Drewes and roos to fret.
For lower land was so admired,
electric companies now vied
to buy Drewe land to build high towers,
to link the cities with their power.
'It must be done,' the Drewes were told,
'before you're even halfway old.
You'll be paid off, gone in an hour.
We need your land to carry power.
And we can make you take our price.
You'll find non-farming life quite nice.'

Oh, what a sadness fell that night
as Farmer Drewe reviewed his plight:
the roos and he no longer neighbours,
or doing one another favours,

or sharing land they both loved well
where splendid evening shadows fell
and made all creatures feel so well —
the roos,
likewise the Drewes.

and in the darkness on the ridge
above the River Carratidge,
the kangaroos remained upright
discussing how to stand and fight,
to save their friends upon the farm
who stood between themselves and harm,
who kept away the men with guns
that shot at roos on other runs.

The joeys even stayed up too,
watching as discussion flew
between the older kangaroos,
the senior males and females who
were leaders of the tribes of roo.
'He'll hate it in the city too,'
said one extremely wise old roo.
'He's likely to get very blue.

This is great country we all share,
the trees are tall, the weather's fair.
The ancestors we never knew,
and ancestors of Roger Drewe,
they lie here too.
To send him to another part,
it will, I tell you, break his heart.
If we're to save this place, our dream,
we'll have to find a clever scheme.'

Late that night in Cudgedong,
strange shadows flitted right along
the tree-lined pavements wide and long.

Outside the shoe store of May Strong
they stopped and hummed a little song,
a song to keep the town asleep,
to keep the townsfolk snoring deep.

Now kangaroos can open doors
by concentrating on their paws —
they do so only for good cause.
They concentrate in threes and fours,
and, by and by, there go the doors!
As did the door of May Strong's store.

he oldest kanga wrote a note:
'Dear Mrs Strong, we took a vote.
We'd like to buy your total stock
(except the frilly little frock).
We need your shoes for honest use,
and we're all set to pay our dues,
so here's my golden credit card.
Please use it with our best regard.
And just to show we mean no harm,
accept this jar of kanga balm
to help your skin.
You'll be like kin.'

ow, when the Drewes looked out at dawn
across the frosty morning lawn,
they saw a thing you never would!
Below the ridge the roos all stood
on tiptoe, shoes on lower paws,
against the normal kanga laws,
that said a roo should never use
a shoe.

When men turned up to build the towers
the roos had stood there for some hours.
Joeys in sneakers, roos in pumps
or cocktail shoes with glistening rumps,
or boots designed for riding horses
or hiking to the Snowy's sources.

and Roger Drewe, he said, 'My friends,
you'll hurt yourself for no good end.
I have to go, I can't remain,
so please don't cause yourself such pain.'

the oldest roo replied outright,
'We are your brothers in this fight,
we mean to show that roos in shoes
are no more likely to bemuse,
or seem ridiculous to man,
than building towers on your land.
There's no excuse for roos in shoes,
and none for tower-building crews,
on land belonging to the Drewes.

And we will wear our sneakers, pumps,
our cocktail shoes with glistening rumps,
our boots designed for riding horses
or hiking to the Snowy's sources,
until the tower builders wilt,
and leave their towers all un-built.
Till we are left just as we choose:
above – the roos; below – the Drewes.'

the tower builders did their best,
but could not work with any zest
when watched by lines of roos in shoes,
and, in time, by TV crews

who filmed the lines of shoe-girt kangas
standing politely, with their banners:
'THEY SHOULD BE KEPT TO LIVE WITH ROOS!'
'THEY SHOULD BE LET LIVE WHERE THEY CHOOSE!'

LIVE WITH ROOS!
LET LIVE WHERE THEY CHOOSE!

And people came to cheer the roos,
at first in merely ones and twos,
and then in crowds who lined the fence,
and thought it made the plainest sense
for kanga folk to guard their land,
and make this most amusing stand.

One day Prime Minister Anne Adair
arrived along with daughter, Clair.
They saw the roos in solemn lines
wearing their finest number nines.
Clair turned to her quite famous mother
and said, 'Now listen, Mum, I'd rather
see these towers all torn down,
and put much further out of town.
Somewhere that won't upset these creatures,
somewhere that doesn't have such features
as Drewes,
and roos in shoes.'

What could she say, PM Adair,
a woman wanting to be fair,
who said she had a special care
for native beasts and bushland rare?
And while the cities were electric
and needed power fast and hectic,
she thought that here on the Drewes' farm,
the towers did not good, but harm.

She called her ministers to meet,
and by the fence along the street
they voted in a solid bloc
in favour of the kanga flock.

Now at this news the Drewes shed tears,
and served the tower builders beers.

As for the painfully shod roos,
they seemed to need no further clues.
They all launched into kanga song
about the land where they belong,
removed their shoes and sang along.
So did May Strong.

the story might have ended then,
and I could put away my pen,
except for Edouard de Gruse,
who read within the evening news
the poignant tale of roos in shoes.

De Gruse, a well-known stage director,
tracked the roos to their own sector
and said, 'What gifts you roos possess!
Such huge potential to impress!
I can see your names in lights:
"Roos in Shoes", full every night.
And you'd be famous, make your millions,
living your lives in grand pavilions.'

The roos said, 'Thank you, Edouard,
but we would find it very hard.
For we're not freaks, we're simply roos.
The only reason we wore shoes
was for the love of our dear Drewes.
Theatres aren't the place for us,
we don't like all that noise and fuss.
We're happy right here where we are,
the farm below, the ridges far.'

nd so the roos proved yet again,
the finest thing for beast and man
is to be faithful to your friends.

They put on shoes not for the fame,
and not to play some silly game,
but simply to save Farmer Drewe.
Those roos,
who once wore shoes.